One Day at a Time
The Tale of Nervous Nell

To the memory of Bill W.
—M.H.
For Jules and Jim
—B. McN.

Text copyright © 1996 by Margaret Hopkins.
Illustrations copyright © 1996 by Bruce McNally.
All rights reserved. Published by Scholastic Inc.
CARTWHEEL BOOKS and the CARTWHEEL BOOKS logo
are registered trademarks of Scholastic Inc.

Library of Congress Cataloging-in-Publication Data

Hopkins, Margaret.
    One day at a time : the tale of nervous Nell / by Margaret Hopkins :
illustrated by Bruce McNally.
        p.   cm. — (One day at a time)
    "Cartwheel Books."
    Summary: Nell, a worrisome chicken, is nervous during her entire
vacation, but her friend Jane reassures her and comforts her throughout
the trip.
    ISBN 0-590-26593-8
    [1. Chickens—Fiction. 2. Vacations—Fiction. 3. Self-esteem—
Fiction.] I. McNally, Bruce, ill. II. Title. III. Series: Hopkins, Margaret. One
day at a time.
PZ7.H777On 1996   95-10286
[E]—dc20   CIP
                                                                                AC

12 11 10 9 8 7 6 5 4 3 2 1   6 7 8 9/9 0 1/0

Printed in the U.S.A.   24
First Scholastic printing, March 1996

One Day at a Time
The Tale of Nervous Nell

by Margaret Hopkins • Illustrated by Bruce McNally

Cartwheel
·B·O·O·K·S·®

SCHOLASTIC INC.
New York   Toronto   London   Auckland   Sydney

It was summer, and the chicken yard at Flatbrook Farm was hot and crowded. The hens meant to be polite to each other, but it was like walking on eggshells. Someone's beak was always out of joint.

"Watch out for my chick!" clucked a mother hen.

"Don't raise your hackle feathers with me!" cried another.

One morning the farmer's son left the gate to the yard open by mistake. Most of the chickens paid no attention, but a bold Rhode Island Red named Jane raced to the gate and peeked out.

"Wonderful!" she said to herself. "I can get out of this crowded yard for a while. I'll go on a little vacation. Maybe Nell will come with me."

Jane's friend Nell agreed to go. But Nell began to worry about the trip, even before it started.

"I'll try to be a good travel companion, Jane," said Nell, her wattles shaking nervously. "But why do we have to go?"

Jane's answer was full of grit. "Those who do not venture forth have no adventures!" said she.

Jane put on the doll hat that she used as a bonnet. Then she was ready to leave. Several friends gathered around to say good-bye.

Vain Marlene shook her pretty brown head. "Don't go!" she said. "Travel will be hard on your feathers."

"Don't go!" said a speckled hen named Betty. "It takes money to travel. You need a nest egg."

A sweet little Bantam hen named Wilhelmina covered her eyes. "I won't be able to sleep a wink until you're home again," she said. "Go safely, dear friends."

Jane and Nell started down the dusty road away from the farm. Soon they saw water.

"This is a river," said Jane. "If we stay by the river, we can't get lost. When it's time to go home, we'll just follow the river back."

It sounded simple, but Nell's poor chicken heart was pounding.

Nell had never been away from Flatbrook Farm before. She sat down in the middle of the road and began to cry.

"I can't go on this trip!" she wailed. "Something terrible might happen. What if it rains tonight? What if the river overflows tomorrow? What if there's a mudslide after that?"

"Nell, you mustn't worry so," Jane told her friend. "Just think about one day at a time. For today, we're fine. It's a warm summer morning. It isn't raining. The river isn't rising. In fact, the world is absolutely Grade A."

Soon Jane calmed Nell, and they began walking down the road again.

As Jane suggested, the two friends kept the river on their left and their eyes on the road. They stopped now and then for a drink from the river and a fresh bug to eat.

"Buck-buck!" The sound of their happy chatter filled the summer air.

Then they came to a muddy section of the road. Nell immediately forgot it was a wonderful day.

"Oh no! Oh no!" she cried. "What shall we do?"

"We'll walk carefully around one mud hole at a time," said Jane. "Follow me, Nell."

Jane slowly picked her way around one boggy hole after another, with Nell squishing along behind.

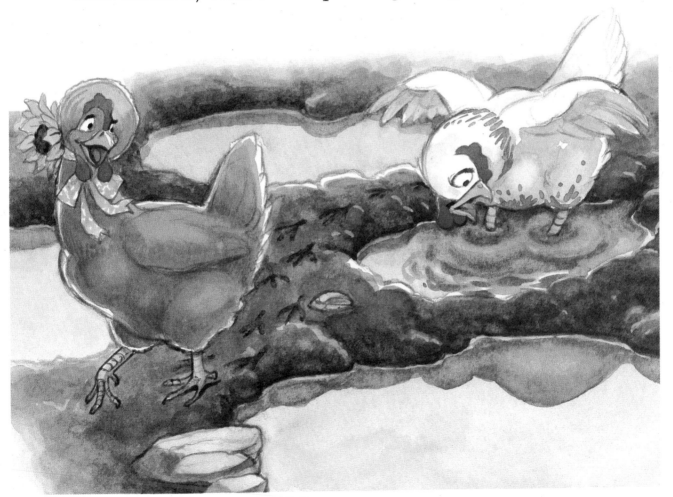

That afternoon Nell stumbled on a round piece of metal lying in the road. There was a picture on it.

Nell stared at the picture. "Oh no!" she cried. "It's one of our enemies! It's an eagle!"

"It's money," said Jane. "Betty said we need money for our trip. We'll take the coin with us."

Jane took off her bonnet and slipped the coin inside. Nell didn't think they should be carrying the picture of an eagle with them, but she trusted Jane and went along.

As they roosted by the river that night, Nell began to worry again.

"What if we come to a fork in the river tomorrow?" said Nell nervously, her poor wattles shivering in the night air. "We won't know which way to go. Jane, we should start home first thing in the morning."

"Dear Nell, stop!" said Jane. "Remember, it's one day at a time. Don't borrow trouble from tomorrow. For tonight, we are fine. The moon is out, and the river is sparkling. We'll know what to do tomorrow when we get there."

Jane said the next day would be Jumbo Grade A, and it was. In the morning she and Nell found a log lying in the path. They hopped on and rolled down the road together, giggling all the way.

Late in the day, they came to the edge of a cornfield.
It was a fine spot to have supper.

"Time to eat," said Nell.

"No one will have to egg me on," said Jane.
"And that's no yolk!"

The two hens laughed and laughed.

But late that night, Nell grew nervous all over again.

"Jane!" she whispered as they settled into their nightly river roost. "What if a fox finds us? Oh, Jane, we'd better get up and start home this minute!"

"Wait, Nell," said Jane, holding her friend back. "There haven't been foxes in this part of the country in years. If you're still nervous in the morning, we can start back. But we don't have to decide tonight."

Nell settled down, and before long the two chickens dozed off into feathery dreams.

The next day wasn't Grade A. Nell had the feeling that they were in danger, and even Jane felt uneasy.

"There's a fox around here somewhere!" said Nell, her beady eyes glancing up and down the road. "Jane, let's go home."

Before Jane could answer, a big hound dog appeared out of nowhere and raced toward them.

"Run, Nell, run!" Jane shouted.

Off they raced. The hound chased the two chickens until finally each one jumped into a low tree— where the dog couldn't reach them.

Even after the dog gave up and went away, poor tired Nell sat in the tree weeping. "We'll never make it home!" she cried. "We're done for, Jane."

"No, we're not," said Jane, bravely jumping out of the tree and straightening her feathers. "I'm not ready to give up."

Jane looked all around, trying to get her bearings. Suddenly her little eyes grew large. "Take a look at this sign, Nell," she said excitedly. "We've seen it before. We've *been* here before!"

PRIVATE
NO
FISHING

"We're home!" shouted Nell. "We made it, Jane!"

It was true. The two chickens hadn't spent their vacation walking along a river's edge. They had been walking around a lake. They had gone full circle and were back where they had started ... at Flatbrook Farm.

The two happy friends ran lickety-split to their old henhouse. The farmer's son saw them coming and opened the gate to the yard.

Everyone welcomed them back. Betty gave Jane a peck on the cheek. Jane gave Betty the coin that she and Nell had found.

"Here's a nest egg for you," said Jane. "Now you can go on a trip, too."

"What a good idea!" said Betty. "But what if it's not enough money? What if I fall down and break a leg and—"

Nell interrupted. "There's only one way to go on a trip or to do most anything — and that's one day at a time, Betty. If you stick with today, your trip will be . . .

absolutely GRADE A!"